Busy-Busy Little Chick

Janice N. Harrington

Busy-Busy

For Anna I. Day —J.N.H.

To my busy-busy Chloe and Dobbin —B.P.

Farrar Straus Giroux Books for Young Readers
175 Fifth Avenue, New York 10010

Text copyright © 2013 by Janice N. Harrington
Pictures copyright © 2013 by Brian Pinkney
Color separations by Bright Arts (HK) Ltd.
Printed in China by South China Printing Co. Ltd.,
Dongguan City, Guangdong Province
First edition, 2013
10 9 8 7 6 5 4 3 2 1

mackids.com

Library of Congress Cataloging-in-Publication Data
Harrington, Janice N.
    Busy-busy Little Chick / Janice Harrington ; pictures by Brian Pinkney.
  — 1st ed.
        p.   cm.
    Summary: Mama Nsoso knows her chicks need a warm new house, but each day
when they set out to collect sticks and mud she is distracted by good things to eat,
while Little Chick stays busy gathering the building materials himself.
    ISBN 978-0-374-34746-8 (hardcover)
    [1. Perseverance (Ethics)—Fiction.   2. Chickens—Fiction.]   I. Pinkney, J. Brian, ill.   II. Title.

PZ7.H23815Bus 2013
[E]—dc23

Little Chick

Pictures by Brian Pinkney

Farrar Straus Giroux
New York

Mama Nsoso's chicks shivered in their cold, damp nest.

"*Peo-peo*, Mama. *Peo-peo*. We're chilly-cold. Our tummies are chilly-cold. Our feet are chilly-cold. We're chilly-cold *all* over."

And Little Chick said, "Mama, my bottom is chilly-cold. *Peo-peo-peo*."

Mama Nsoso spread her wings around her children. "Don't worry, my babies," she said. "When morning comes, we will build an ilombe, a new house. It will have a grass roof, mud walls, and a cozy nest inside. The wind will not blow in. The rain will not drip in, and the dark night will not bother us."

Morning came. Mama Nsoso tumbled her babies from the nest. It was time to build their new ilombe. She stepped out and her chicks, *peo-peo*, peeped right behind her. As she walked, she searched for leaves and twigs to build the nest for their new house. She stepped along—*cwa-cwa-cwa*—until she saw

crunchy-munchy,

sweety-meaty,

big fat worms!

"Pruck! Pruck!" clucked Mama Nsoso. "We will work tomorrow. Today we will peck and gobble big fat worms."

But busy-busy Little Chick did not peck worms.

He gathered twigs—*tee-tee-tee*—and he picked leaves—
tee-tee-tee—until his pile grew taller than a pepper bush.

In the evening, Mama Nsoso and her chicks squeezed into their old nest. The wind blew and spilled cool air beneath their feathers. The night fell and left damp dew atop their beaks. Mama Nsoso's babies shivered and shook.

"*Peo-peo*, Mama. *Peo-peo*. We're cold. Our feathers are cold. Our feet are cold. We're cold *all* over."

But Little Chick said nothing at all. He had already fallen asleep, snoring *peeee-ah, peeeeeee-ah*.

Mama Nsoso wrapped her wings around her babies. "Don't worry, my children. When morning comes, we will build a new house. You won't be cold again."

When the sun came up, Mama Nsoso swept her chicks from the nest and together they strutted off—*cwa-cwa-cwa*—to gather leaves and twigs and also grass for the roof of their new ilombe. But just then Mama Nsoso saw

crunchy-munchy,

jumpy-jumpy,

cricky-cracky crickets!

"Pruck! Pruck!" clucked Mama Nsoso. "We will work tomorrow. Today we will munch cricky-cracky crickets."

But busy-busy Little Chick plucked and plucked the long thin grass—
tee-tee-tee.

At last, he'd built a pile as round as a ripe melon.

That night, Mama Nsoso settled into her nest and tucked her head beneath her wing. Her babies snuggled close against her soft, soft feathers, but still they could not sleep. The wind swooshed and made them cold. The damp air clung to their feathers. The dark-dark surrounded their nest and made them shiver.

Her babies huddled beneath her wings. *"Peo-peo-peo,"* they cried.

"Don't worry," said Mama Nsoso. "Tomorrow we will build a new ilombe. It will be warm and dry and as large as my wings spread wide-wide."

But Little Chick said nothing at all. He had fallen asleep, snoring *peeeeee-ah, peeeeee-ah, peeee-ah.*

In the morning, Mama Nsoso and her babies left the nest to gather leaves and twigs and grass—and also mud for the walls of their new ilombe. The chicks stepped—*cwa-cwa-cwa*—and strutted—*cwa-cwa-cwa*—until Mama squawked, "*Bala! Bala!* Look! Look!"

Round-brown,

roasty-roasty,

picky-pecky corn!

"Pruck! Pruck!" said Mama Nsoso. "We will work tomorrow. Today we will peck and gobble this tasty corn."

But busy-busy Little Chick did not peck for corn. Instead—*tee-tee-tee*—he scratched and scraped up gooey mud all by himself.

All by himself, he piled the mud beside the grass, beside the twigs and leaves.

He scraped and
piled all day long.

Mama Nsoso gathered her babies and settled them into the old nest. The wind slithered in. The damp oozed in, and the dark coiled around the sides of the nest and made them shiver.

"Mama, Mama," her babies cried. "We want a new ilombe!"

"Don't worry, my poor babies," clucked Mama Nsoso. "Tomorrow we will build a new ilombe. Tomorrow we will have a new house."

Little Chick said nothing. He was tired, tired, tired, *peee-ah, peeee-ah.*

The next morning, Mama Nsoso woke up in the old nest. Her feathers were ruffled and damp. She was cold and stiff. And the nest was—empty!

Mama Nsoso searched for her babies until she heard, "*Peo-peo-peo!* Mama! *Peo-peo!*"

Beside a tall tree she saw a beautiful new ilombe. It was as large as her wings spread wide-wide. It had smooth mud walls, a green grassy roof, a clean leafy nest, and baby chicks running in and out.

"Mama, Mama," they cheeped. "Our new house! It's not cold, it's not wet, and it's not dark and scary."

The new ilombe was just right.

"It looks *per-per-perfect*!" clucked Mama. "But who built such a lovely ilombe? Who gathered the twigs and the leaves and the grass and the mud?"

"It was Little Chick!" the other chicks said.

"Pruck! Pruck! Pruckkkk!" Mama Nsoso clucked with pride.

But Little Chick said nothing at all. He was busy-busy chasing cricky-cracky crickets all by himself!

Author's Note

Busy-Busy Little Chick is based on the fable "The Hen's House," told by the Nkundo people of Central Africa. The fable appears in Alice D. Cobble's *Wembi, the Singer of Stories* (St. Louis, Mo.: Bethany Press, 1959). Cobble was a missionary at the Monieka Mission in what is now the Democratic Republic of the Congo. At the mission, Cobble collected stories from the Nkundo people, who spoke the Lonkundo language. She writes that the stories "were really told and retold to us by countless numbers of Africans. Some were told patiently, sentence by sentence, at a time when we were not too familiar with their speech; later, others were brought in by a few of the students who heard that we were interested; still others were recounted to my husband as he spent many, many long evenings out in the villages."

Although Cobble's work provided the inspiration, I drew on *"On Another Day . . .": Tales Told Among the Nkundo of Zaïre*, by Mabel H. Ross and Barbara K. Walker (Hamden, Conn.: Archon Books, 1979), which discusses Cobble's work and offers more description of Nkundo storytelling and culture.

I have tried to shape a tale that evokes the traditional storytelling of the Nkundo but remains an original interpretation by an American storyteller.

Additional information about the Monieka Mission and the work of Cobble and her husband can be found in Donald Burke's article, "Congo Mission," in *Life* (June 1947): 105–13.

Another useful source is *English-Lonkundo and Lonkundo-English Vocabulary* (Bolenge, Belgian Congo: Foreign Christian Missionary Society, 1913). Online edition: http://www.archive.org/details/englishlonkundol00boleuoft.

Glossary

Busy-Busy Little Chick uses words and storytelling traditions from the Nkundo people of Central Africa. The Nkundo speak the Lonkundo language.

bala (**bah**-lah) is a Lonkundo word that means "look" or "behold."

cwa-cwa-cwa (**chwa-chwa-chwa**) is used to show Mama Nsoso and her chicks walking from place to place. Nkundo storytellers repeat the expression *cwa* to show two companions walking together and moving forward. It is another way of saying "going, going."

ilombe (ee-**lom**-bay) is a Lonkundo word that means "house."

nsoso (en-**so**-so) is a Lonkundo word that means "chicken."

tee-tee-tee (tay-tay-tay) is used by Nkundo storytellers to suggest an action that goes on and on.